D0991521

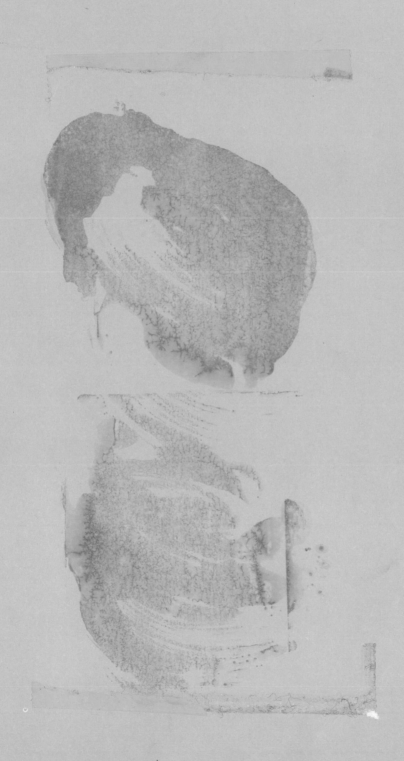

TIM AND JIM

Claire Schumacher

DODD, MEAD & COMPANY
New York

Juv/E
Fic

For

Eudes
Tiphaine
Alice
Jean-Brice
and Luçie

R0061579957

Copyright © 1987 by Claire Schumacher. All rights reserved. No part of this book may be reproduced in any form without permission in writing from the publisher. Distributed in Canada by McClelland and Stewart Limited, Toronto. Printed in Hong Kong by South China Printing Company.

Design by Sylvia Frezzolini

1 2 3 4 5 6 7 8 9 10

Library of Congress Cataloging-in-Publication Data
Schumacher, Claire.   Tim and Jim.   Summary: Tim is a happy cat in his cozy little house, except for wanting a friend. Jim is a street cat who longs for a warm home. [1. Cats — Fiction]
I. Title.   PZ7.S3914Ti 1987   [E]   87-475
ISBN 0-396-09040-0

TIM AND JIM

Tim was a beautiful orange and white cat. He lived with Miss Periwinkle in a cozy little house.

Miss Periwinkle loved Tim very much and took good care of him. She always brought him the best cat food and treats.

Every evening Tim sat in the window and waited
for Miss Periwinkle to come home from work.

She greeted him happily, "Hello, Tim!
I went shopping for you."

Tim jumped up to look in the bag.
There was no friend inside, just food and treats.
She had forgotten AGAIN!

MEOW

MEOW

"Don't be so impatient,
Tim," said Miss Periwinkle.
"Here is your dinner."

MEOW

But Tim was not hungry,
he kept complaining.

MEOW

MEOW

"What's the matter?" Miss Periwinkle said, hugging and kissing him. "You have everything!" Indeed, Tim was a very lucky cat.

Not far away, a street cat named Jim was searching
for food in a garbage can. He looked just like Tim except
he had a black patch on his ear.

"If only I could live in one of those warm houses and
have somebody to love me," he thought.

That night poor Jim slept on the cold hard ground, dreaming of a better life.

Meanwhile, Tim was sleeping comfortably on
Miss Periwinkle's bed, dreaming of the friend he longed for.

The next morning, Tim made up his mind. "I'm tired of waiting! I'm going out to find a friend!" He slipped through an open window, knocking Miss Periwinkle's glasses to the floor....

Tim walked down the street until he came upon a cat
perched on a fence. "Will you be my friend?" he asked.

But this cat was not at all friendly. "Get lost!" he snarled. "Or else I'll give you a scratch you will never forget!"

Tim barely escaped.

He was so scared, he kept running and running,
so fast and so far that he completely lost his way.

"Where am I?" he cried. "I want to go home."

Miss Periwinkle looked everywhere for Tim, but all she found were her broken glasses.

"Oh, Tim! Where are you hiding? Have you run away? Please come back! I promise I won't be angry."

But Tim couldn't hear her. He was too far away.

Miss Periwinkle decided to make posters to help find Tim.

"I do wish I had my glasses!" she sighed.

She hung the posters all over the neighborhood.
Just as she put up the last one, it started to rain.

"What a terrible storm!" said Miss Periwinkle.
"I hope my poor Tim is all right!"

In fact, Tim was having a very bad time. He was
soaking wet.

Jim was used to such storms and knew how to take
care of himself. He quickly took shelter in a mailbox.

When the rain stopped,
the mailman found Jim.
"Look what's in here!
You must be the lost cat
on the posters."

"Come with me,
I'll give you a ride
home."

"Tim! Thank goodness, you're back!" cried Miss Periwinkle, as the mailman handed Jim to her.

"You must be hungry!" she said, and she gave Jim all of Tim's favorite treats.

"I see you've lost your collar. Never mind, I'll buy you a new one tomorrow, when I go to get my glasses fixed."

As darkness fell, Tim
was still walking,
searching for his house.
Finally, things looked
familiar again....

"This is MY STREET!
That is MY HOUSE!"
he cried, and ran to the
door. It was locked.

Inside the house Jim couldn't believe his good luck.
It was so comfortable and warm on this nice lady's bed.
"At last," he purred, "I've found someone to love me!"
"I'm so glad to have you back," said Miss Periwinkle,
stroking his head. Suddenly they heard loud MEOWS
outside. Miss Periwinkle sat up.
"My goodness! That sounds like Tim! But how can
that be? You are here on my bed!"

Then there was a scratching at the door. Miss Periwinkle
went downstairs and opened it. Tim jumped into her arms.

He purred loudly. Miss Periwinkle saw Tim's collar.
"YOU ARE TIM!" she exclaimed. "Then WHO is upstairs?"

Jim wondered what was going on, and came down
the stairs. "Oh no, another cat! Will the lady still keep me?"

At that moment Tim saw Jim.
"Wow!" he meowed. "This is
just what I wanted —A FRIEND!

Will you play with me?"
he asked Jim.

Tim and Jim started to play.
Miss Periwinkle was puzzled.
"I lost one cat, and now I have two!
What shall I do?"

Of course she kept them both.